Praise for Ted Krever's books:

Swindler & Son

'Exhilarating'

'I read the first hundred pages without coming up for air.'

'...smart, energetic, wryly funny and full of delightfully unexpected plot twists. Nicky Sandler...is humble, mad-brainy, loyal and a ninja-master of getting over...I loved this book from the first page to the last.'

'...zippy and funny...inventive and entertaining...'

'clever, dark and gripping to the end..."Madcap? Maybe. Zany? Yes. Frantic? Definitely. Entertaining? Oh yeah!'

Swindler & Son 2: 100% Genuine Forgeries!!

'A comedy heist with a little romance and lots of justice - at the end, of course.'

A Novel for Now

'Writing in this American era where both halves of the voting public believe the other half is promoting a con, Krever returns with his full speed mix of one liners, global plot twists, and cast of genial art forgery con artists…high stakes global money laundering and assassination attempts, where only honest swindlers can figure out how to outplay the bigger swindlers and survive…the page turning fun gains depth with reflections about memory, honesty, reality, social trust, truth, humanity, authenticity, and art. No spoiler alerts except this: the biggest cons have consequences, true friendship in the end relies on a moral center..' (Five Stars)

'Such Fun!

'If you enjoy a good romp through the art world (of which I know nothing but loved learning about) then this is the book for you! Nicky and Harry have worked together before (in book 1) and are very good at forging paintings to rake in a small fortune. But this sequel has an unexpected twist that you won't see coming! Set in several places--including Moscow--this is a wild ride and a caper like you've never experienced before! So be prepared to set aside adulting for a while and just immerse yourself in this plot with wildly quirky characters and a great plot!' (Four Stars)

I0621325

Mindbenders

"...a storyline that takes hold in the first few pages and doesn't let go..."
"...really fast paced...I found myself unable to put it back down."

"...dialog that left me breathless."
"...[a] global, international conspiracy of corporate and governmental politics, mind control, murder and intrigue."
"OMG!...finally crawled into bed early hours of the next day."
"This is that rare piece of fiction based on fact in such a way as to make the two seem to blur."
"Mindbenders...will make you wonder if your mind really does belong to you."

Mindbenders 2: The Fiery Sky

"...a more than worthy followup to the 1st book, fast paced, well written and exciting!"
"...takes me places that were only in my imagination - I feel like I have been to that island in the South Pacific living on the water, and I've been parched in the Aussie desert - it's all real."
"...A complete thrill ride from beginning to end...great style and substance."
"...intense, memorable scenes..."
"...seamlessly weaves multiple storylines together, delivering a powerful punch of an ending."

GREEN

"...not your typical romance...
"...a unique look into the mindset of men, rather than the typical romance, which is told from the woman's point of view."
"... a smart, witty and wise look at love later in life..."
"I found myself laughing aloud more than once, only to shortly thereafter find myself deeply touched."
"The descriptions...of Ireland are alone worth the price of the book..."
"If you like reading about horses, Ireland, friendship, love in any form..."
"Part a love story, part a political thriller, and part a satiric commentary on life and politics..."
"Green is a charming book."

Howling at Wolves

"This book, simply put...is funny!"
"Keep your tissues handy as you won't stop laughing."
"Nothing is sacred..."
"...like Garp on steroids (or maybe Viagra?)

A Crafty and Devious God

"...a great read..."

"Weirdly excellent"

"[The] writing is very natural, loose and easy, yet deep and thoughtful."

"...an engaging character study... a tale of a man who's lost, looking for his way, and a girl who knows she is destined for great things and is determined to achieve it at all costs."

"I gave it a try. And kept reading, and reading, and reading. Just very well-written, scattered throughout with concepts that made me think (which I occasionally like to do)."

After

...short stories of New Yorkers trying to make sense of their changed world in the immediate aftermath of 9/11."

"These stories are emotionally impactful but they are not grim. Each character finds some measure of hope or understanding or, at the very least, adaptation to their circumstances."

"...a masterful job of depicting the surreal dream-like state that trauma survivors inhabit..."

"Intricately woven stories of despair and ultimately hope..."

"...a tender tribute to the survivors of 9/11."

Ted Krever

After

by
Ted Krever

Little David Publications
www.tedkrever.com

Ted Krever

ISBN: 978-1-7327865-2-3

~~~~

~~~~

Author's Note

This is a collection of short stories, some of them directly about September 11th, others just reflective of the era. I've included the dates they were originally finished because I find it interesting to see the way perspective changed over time.

~~~

Ted Krever

After

November 9, 2001

I knew something was wrong when I saw the heavy rubber fireman's coat on the couch.

I had been up in Washington Square Park, in the garden of candles, swaying and singing with the crowd, watching people holding each other and standing together, praying in the manner of our 21st Century secular grab-bag religion—a little Christian good faith, a touch of Buddhist stoicism, a dash of Taoist centering, strained through a mesh of Jewish skepticism.

The young people were talking, sharing this experience in the hushed tones they'd previously heard only on golf telecasts, talking with the shock and fresh pain of the uninitiated. I, on the other hand, could tick off without effort Francis Gary Powers

Ted Krever

being shot down, policemen with fire hoses and clubs attacking black people in the streets of Mississippi, Jacqueline Kennedy climbing the trunk of the open limousine, Dr. King on the balcony in Memphis, Bobby Kennedy on the floor of a Los Angeles hotel kitchen, policemen with clubs attacking students in Chicago, Chappaquidick, 4 dead in Ohio, helicopters straining to lift off the roof of our embassy in Saigon with passengers clinging to the skids, Reagan shot, Challenger exploding, Sadat, Indira Gandhi and Yitzhak Rabin. While this shock was deeper and the hole in the skyline much much bigger than I'd ever imagined possible, the shock itself was familiar, the same breathtaking vivid vacuum in my chest that I'd known periodically since childhood. Welcome to the World, kids, I thought condescendingly, and was properly ashamed of myself for it.

So when I got home and saw the fireman's coat, my stomach started growling immediately.

"What's with the coat?" I asked Sam. He was in the kitchen in his underwear drinking beer.

"I got lucky," he said, switching between Conan and some French movie on Bravo. He was watching both simultaneously.

"You used the coat to get laid?" I yelled and he looked over at me like I was some sort of child.

"What is your problem?" he demanded, with the weariness of a combat veteran. Which is obviously what he'd been pretending to be. Sam is the kid who's renting the third bedroom in my apartment since Maura moved out. He was a volunteer fireman in Staten Island before moving to Manhattan—I saw the coat when he first moved in. He promised he'd get me out alive if the building ever caught fire. Now, for the first time in the four months he's lived here, the coat had come out of the closet.

"Did you put charcoal on your face to make it look like you just came from the site?" I continued screaming. "Did you tell her the names of the dead men in your company? Did you tell her how you led people down the stairs and just managed to get that one wheelchair victim out as the tower came down?"

"Off the pedestal, please," he said. "She was upset, she was scared, like everybody else. You think I'm not affected by this? You think I don't have a heart? I wanted to do something. I went down to the site. They said they couldn't take more volunteers right now. They said come back tomorrow. So I'm coming back up here and she's standing on a streetcorner bawling her eyes out. She had three friends who worked there and she'd just gotten off the phone with them, right there on the corner—all alive. They all got out. She needed to be with someone. And so did I, if you want to know the truth. I was really kind of upset they had nothing for me down there. I couldn't stand not doing anything. So we ended up together. I didn't go out looking to fool anybody."

Coming from him, this was an aria of raw emotion. His dullness—his lack of feeling, the old-fashioned John Wayne granite resolve—had struck me from the day he moved in. He had lost his parents just a few months before, and seemed determined not to be touched by anything. Unlike my college roommates—the last time I'd ever *had* roommates—he refused to be drawn into any conversation that involved feelings. He almost appeared to have no personal aspect at all.

I rendered this judgment even though rendering judgments made me uncomfortable, and guilty in some strange way. I grew up in a generation that obsessed over the shallowness, the condescension, the puritanical straitjacket of the idea of judging others, of boiling down another human's hard-fought worldview and putting it on a scale. We believed there was always another mile to be walked in the other guy's shoes. So I tried not to judge Sam harshly for his…whatever it was. Maybe just self-reliance. He was honest, no drugs, a decent roommate who paid his rent on time. Just not particularly blessed—or cursed—with deep feeling. "I'm sorry," I said. "Sorry I went off."

"It's okay," he murmured, opening another beer. "You didn't know. There's probably somebody out there trying that scam right now." He looked over at the coat lying on the couch—I looked at it too.

"So—can I borrow it? Go check out a couple bars?" I asked, and burst out laughing. It felt good to laugh, funny joke or not.

"Absolutely not," he said, laughing too.

I drank too much wine while he finished a six-pack. We saw the end of the French movie—it lasted longer than Conan so we stared at the last twenty minutes without channelswapping, not that either of us could recollect a frame of it after. Then I went off to my room with a view of the lights and the smoke, the noise and the smell from half a mile away. I didn't sleep for a long time. I found myself going through the catalog again, from Francis Gary—a saint's names—to Yitzhak, the litany of impersonal poundings my heart has taken that have never really faded away.

He *did* fool her, I thought. She thought he was from the site. She thought he was one of them. Or maybe it didn't matter, like he said. Maybe she just wanted to be with someone. But that coat was the price of admission, the coat all by itself. That's why there was no pleasure in it for him. That's why he was sitting in the kitchen drinking a six-pack at 1 in the morning. That's why he wasn't still at her place. Bet he doesn't even have her number, I thought. And maybe that's alright with her, too.

I knew I was turning mental cartwheels, but that was nothing new for me. Again, I didn't want to be judgmental, to attach any moral stigma to these thoughts. I wasn't thinking badly of Sam—I was just weighing the scales as some sort of exercise. It was abstract, almost random, but somehow, it felt important to me at the moment. It was something I needed to do. Some impulse was tugging at me, something that felt fresh, that required new muscles to be exercised, muscles I'd neglected for a long time. There was a change of routine here that had less to do with the past than the future, if we had a future.

Sam went back to the site the next day and worked, worked there for over a week. He returned to the apartment every couple of days, and then he'd drink and stare at the television and sleep, which is all anybody could do.

I went to work each day, sprinting from morning to night, putting out the news. I'm an operations executive in the news division of one of the television networks, and all any of us could do at first was try to keep up.

It took several weeks, but we almost regained routine. Every morning on the way to work, I ticked off subway stations and store names and floors on the elevator, listing them for myself by rote, from habit, rebuilding each morning the reassurance of familiarity. We had just enough of a respite to begin to relax.

Then the first anthrax attack hit—at another network. Over the next few days, several networks got the innocuous letters.

I bought a gas mask one afternoon on lunch break, at an odds-and-ends store down the block from the office. Sam laughed when I brought it home. "That's useless," he informed me. "If it's anthrax, all you need is antibiotics anyway. If it's sarin, the mask won't help." He was back at his job by then, at a newsstand in Rockefeller Center—where the first tainted letter had arrived—so he had studied up on the subject.

I tried to keep my mind on subway stations and elevators and the price of overpriced coffee. In time, there were new encouraging signs— my friends began gossiping about each other again, partisan politics returned in fits and starts to Washington, big businesses began poking each other in competition for bailout money. Normalcy was returning, I was able to tell myself, despite the couple of threatening powdery letters received by the competition.

Then I got the phone call.

"Can you come to Don's office?" Don Masters is, of course, our anchor, veteran of thirty years in the news wars, an esteemed journalist, expansive late-night talk show commentator on world affairs, obsessive visitor to tarot and numerology readers and a man who insists on riding the same expensive quarter horse that's thrown him three times and almost killed him once. One approaches Don at the best of times only when summoned, and then discusses only the topics he raises—any other course can quickly throw this very finicky expensive train right off the tracks.

"What's up, Don?" I said, leaning against his doorpost, trying to appear nonchalant.

"Come in," he said tensely, not even pretending to be social. "Close the door."

I settled into the buttery leather chair next to his sea captain's desk, piled with horsy knickknacks and model sailboats, the detritus of a man who always needed to be reminded of his own vitality. Don paced behind the desk for a few moments, his TV-blue shirt open at the collar, the tie—dramatically casual— loose around his neck.

"We need anthrax," he said.

"I'm sorry?"

"All the other networks have anthrax. We're falling behind. Bin Laden's decided we're irrelevant. What's that going to do to us as an organization?"

One of Don's obsessions is his role in the history of the network, his special place in 'the organization.' *The most venerable news organization in the history of television*—he'd learned the phrase so well it rolled off his tongue at the end of every show, and whenever he'd had a few drinks. But I didn't smell alcohol on his breath. It didn't even sound like competition was concerning him at the moment.

"Don, I don't think anyone's keeping score in quite that way," I ventured.

"Don't be naïve," he muttered. "Everything counts. Everything registers somewhere inside the minds of human beings. If the other networks all have anthrax letters and we don't, it diminishes us forever."

"Okay—so what do you have in mind?" I asked, giving him a second chance to state his goal, a chance to back away from what I was afraid he meant.

"We have to get some," he insisted, without a second thought. "We have to find someplace that has some and get it on a letter here. And I think we need to do this today, so it can be discovered no later than tomorrow. We're already lagging behind." He looked at me with the tension I'd seen on his face in national crises when he'd 'taken charge' of the newsroom—not among my favorite memories.

"If I were thinking of myself," he said, "it would be nice if the letter made it as far as my personal assistant. Look at the mileage Brokaw got out of that—it probably bought him five more years in the chair. But I don't want to take chances with anyone's health—they can find it in the mailroom."

"Uh-huh," I stammered, because I couldn't think of another reply. "Have you talked to anyone else about this? Anybody from upstairs?"

"No," he said, wheeling around from the window and leaning over the desk. "And neither will you. This is not an operation anyone can know about. I don't know about it and neither does anyone else. Neither do *you*, for that matter. As long as you get some powder and get it on a letter, nobody ever has to know anything about it. You drive out to Trenton and mail it tonight. I know a doctor who'll give you Cipro today—you can say you're nervous, working at a network. Tomorrow you'll look like a genius."

I could see he was serious. But apparently he wasn't sure yet that I saw it, or that I was clear as to just *how* serious he was.

"I'll break you," he said, "if you speak about this with anyone."

This was no idle threat, coming from Don Masters. He'd done it before—everyone knew the stories.

In the past ten years, as the world have become ever more centered around the United States, Don Masters had become ever more centered around Don Masters. He threw fits over promos that didn't include his picture in the first two seconds. He remade the set of the Seven o'clock News twice at the advice of his numerologist, with 7's (for success) and 9's (for profundity) stitched into the pattern of the chairs. This was fine until the late 90's, when we had to prepare for HDTV and the engineers found that the pattern could now actually be read—by the three civilians in the country with an HDTV set and sending station. Nonetheless, this required another set rebuild, with smaller and more obscured numbers still present in the stitching.

And the piece de resistance was surely the news magazine piece that required a new voiceover during Don's monthlong vacation in the Hamptons. Don refused to come back to town, even when the network proffered a helicopter to make the trip quicker. Instead, he forced the brass to send a mobile recording truck three hours out to the tip of Long Island, to camp outside a local radio station in order to re-voice his 3 minutes of track. And every time Don was unhappy about something, not only did he get his way, but someone lost their job.

I wondered sometimes if he didn't pay people to repeat these stories in the halls—they did a lot to bolster his reputation, and the reputation of having such power *conferred* that power. I'd been with the organization myself for twenty years—I had a pension and child support payments—it was hard to think of leaving, and especially to go out over *this*.

And when I started looking at things his way, he actually had a point: the lack of a letter *did* make us look bad. We'd been lagging in the ratings for several years, our demographics showed our audience getting progressively older—and now this. I found myself wondering at the fact that I hadn't thought about it myself. I assumed we could weather this storm—the only network not to receive an anthrax letter—but maybe I *was* being naïve. At the same instant this thought occurred to me, it struck me as rank insanity. Hannah Arendt would have a field day here, I thought.

I needed to think. I needed to get out of the office. Besides, even if I decided to do it, how the hell was I going to get ahold of anthrax? On a few hours' notice? I searched my memory for scientists who might work with the stuff—friends of Maura's or people I'd interviewed over the years. It was all a blur. And something was nagging at me, some impulse in my chest that felt off-kilter, like a drumbeat that's a half-step off.

After prowling the halls aimlessly for ten minutes, I decided to talk to Sam. He was a disinterested party and an honest man. He'd keep his mouth shut, come hell or high water, and he wasn't a judgmental sort, not one to take positions or draw moral distinctions at such a time. He'd fooled the girl with his fireman's jacket, after all. He'd listen, I'd talk, and I'd figure out what to do. And then he'd forget it, go home, watch movies on television and drink beer and not bother me about this ever again. Maybe, with luck, he'd know someone who had some anthrax.

I went to Rockefeller Center, to his newsstand, but he wasn't there. The owner of the newsstand said he'd gone home sick. The owner stood in a corner of the tiny cubicle in front of a stack of yesterday's newspapers. He was short, swarthy, mustached and accented—Lebanese? Afghan, maybe?

I scanned the wall racks. I hadn't read a magazine in a month. Now I saw all the special issues, the pictures I'd seen before, many I hadn't. The owner held up one commemorative issue to me. "You want this one?" he said.

"Yes, that's what I was looking for," I told him. It was the magazine we read in my parent's home thirty-five years ago, when my litany of bad memories started. Now it was a comfort to see the disturbing pictures beneath the familiar banner.

He held the magazine up for me, but before I could take it, he pulled it back and opened to one of the center pages, the centerfold with the graphic of the Trade Center, the trajectory of the planes, the timeline of their impact and the general geography we all know so well.

He pointed to the base, the ground floor, of Tower 2. "I worked here," he said, chewing on the words a bit. "I worked the newsstand here," he said, pointing again. I knew that stand, one of the biggest downtown. I'd probably given him money many times. "I was there when it hit," he said. "I was fixing up my stack," and at first I didn't understand what he meant. Then I looked at the pile of newspapers in front of him, the banners cut off for return to the jobber. He'd been preparing his merchandise for return.

"I stayed," he continued. "I heard the noise but I fixed my stack. Then I closed up." There was no irony in his voice, no self-reproach. It's just the way things happened. It was like, all these weeks later, he still had to tell the story in order to discover what he thought about it himself.

"I headed this way," he said, still with the diagram, pointing at a doorway now. "They stopped me—they said 'No— can't go this way. Go over there.' So I go over there. Ten minutes later, I'm back at the same place. I made a circle. I go outside, and the whole thing comes down. Dark cloud all over, in my face in my eyes my mouth my nose. I can't breathe to speak." He opens his mouth and puts his hand in, hands as scoops. He moves them in and out of his mouth a few times, showing me how he worked to be able to breathe again. "I scoop the dust out. Then I yell 'HELP!!' A man comes—fireman—from ten feet away. He takes me. His head is bleeding—my head is bleeding, my shoulder is bleeding. His blood is on my shirt, here on the shoulder. I can't wash it now."

They took him to Liberty State Park, he said, for hospital. Then, when they found out he had no way to return to Brooklyn, the police drove him to a New Jersey police garrison, where other policemen drove him to Brooklyn. That was nice of them, he said. He didn't expect such courtesy from policemen, especially in New Jersey.

"My shoulder still hurts," he says. "I can't lift heavy weight now."

"But you're here," I said.

"I'm here," he repeated, hollowvoiced and paused for a moment, staring out into the busy lobby. "I have a friend, he got a job in the restaurant on the Tower, at the top? His first day—" he stopped.

"That was his first day?"

He nodded. "His first day. He's gone." He was staring at me, without visible feeling, with no response to what he had just said, looking at me as though I could tell him what he should feel, what he should do.

I had nothing to say. I could feel those unfamiliar muscles flexing inside me, those inactive muscles that needed exercise. I could feel them working away, but to no end I could determine as yet. Considering the mission I was on, I was in no position to tell anyone which way was up.

He went back to doing what he could do, all he knew to do at the moment. Six weeks after his world exploded, he was back at work, slitting the banners off the tops of newspapers, slitting them with a boxcutter.

I watched him, watched the blade—almost a visual pun— for what seemed like several minutes. Then I walked back across town, tasting the air and the smells of the city. I went up the elevator and walked right into Don's office.

"We shouldn't do this," I said to Don.

"No?" he said. "And why not?" His mouth was working and his eyebrows got that twitch I'd seen every once in a while during major breaking news stories. We'd even sent him to a consultant several years earlier to try to get control of it, but to no avail. Now I took it as a hopeful sign, that maybe he was feeling a little pressure from me, from inside himself, from some memory or dormant feeling that might now be nagging at him.

"Because it's *wrong*. Because it's a bad idea." I paused, to see if the words might penetrate. They felt funny coming out of my mouth. I wondered when I'd last used the word 'wrong' in adult conversation—clearly, it had been a long time.

Don was chewing on this, but it was clearly a battle for him, a battle against at least ten years of his own history, his comfort level of familiarity and routine and certain levels of authority he'd worked hard for. I decided it would be better not to wait for him to come to a conclusion.

"Besides," I said, looking him firmly in the eye, "it betrays a lack of faith in the organization."

He stiffened at this. "What do you mean?"

"It's *there*, Don," I told him. "It's in our mailroom. It's probably addressed to you. Somebody down there just bungled it. They put it in the wrong pile. If they go looking for it, they'll find it."

I could see his jaw stiffen. I could see the old resolve return, the pride and bravado that made him accept the anchor job in the first place, back when he was a field reporter who didn't want to get stuck behind a desk.

"You're right," he said. "Can you make that happen?"

"Sure," I said. I called the mailroom and told them to initiate a complete search of the entire facility, with workers wearing protective gloves, and to call the instant they found anything suspicious.

And of course, it *was* there. It was even addressed to Don, like I'd promised. I was surprised to see how many executives around the office seemed heartened by this news. They called a press conference immediately to make the announcement. We might have been last, but we were still in the game.

When I went home that night, Sam was on the couch, flipping the channels. A very pretty young woman was feeding him soup.

"I pick up the shipments in the mailroom," he explained. "I tested positive today—they think some of the powder got on a pile of newspapers. So I'm taking Cipro. Shouldn't you?" he asked. He looked positively chipper about it. The girl kept bringing soup from the kitchen.

I must have had a look on my face. "What?" Sam demanded.

I went back to my room and looked out the window. The smoke was gone now, though I knew I'd see it out my window again sometime. I could feel those muscles working inside again, working hard now, trying to get accustomed, trying to achieve the level of familiarity, of routine.

Sam came into my room with the girl.

"I'm moving out," he said. "You've changed."

I nodded and helped them call a cab. Then I went back to watching out the window, watching where the smoke used to be.

Missing

May 6, 2004

The Halls of Justice looked like white whales in a winter storm. Superior Court, Family Court, Hall of Records. Chalky-coated and glinting dull, they loom ghastly against the charcoal clouds. No other footsteps echo the square. No other faces in sight, just a few slim forms on the balconies and rooftops of Chinatown staring south, staring downtown like everyone else in the world.

I'm going to Chinatown. That's the address on the card in the wallet in my jacket pocket.

There are newspapers blowing around the street, though it doesn't feel like a breeze anywhere else. There was a primary today. Did I vote? One more question I can't answer. One of many. Maybe I'll know more at the office.

At the office. The phrase feels familiar. I worked at an office. But this one? We'll see. See if it looks familiar when I open the door.

Even Chinatown is deserted. A few men in their white shirts, slacks and aprons stand around the doorways. Every eye strains above street level, watching the clouds, the clouds from downtown.

The keys in my pants pocket don't fit the street door. But the ones in the jacket pocket do. The dimpled key on the same ring fits the deadbolt of Room 306. Ned Schindler, Investigator. That would be me, I suppose. I've got the keys. I've got the wallet.

It doesn't look familiar, but not much does. I know New York. But then, I could be a tourist from Salt Lake City and know what New York looks like, even today, even on the day when it least looks like itself. But I knew this was Chinatown before I could read the signs. I knew how to find Mott Street. I know Little Italy is a few blocks away. I can distinguish the subway tokens in my pocket from the change. So I know the city. There's just nothing anywhere that feels like *mine*.

Drawers locked. The small key on the jacket ring opens it. It's a top drawer. Files and pens, envelopes and candy, a hundred notes on scrap paper, a few dollars and a few photos and a few more keys.

I leaned back in the seat and then it was morning. Light was pouring in the windows, I could hear at least a few people on the street chattering in Cantonese and I was stiff as a board when I got up.

I looked at the room for signs of the owner. A few photos but totally generic—a zeppelin over the Empire State Building before the TV antenna spire, an autographed picture of Keith Hernandez in Mets blue and orange and a certificate of completion of the Investigator's Preparedness Program in Drug Recognition and Compliance at SUNY Downstate. I'm not connecting with any of this. Now in the light of morning, I see the small television wedged into the middle of a bookshelf. I turn it on and of course it's full of the hole in the city, the hole downtown, the hole that created the cloud.

I came from there. I don't have to watch this to know that. Watching doesn't help though—nothing gets clearer. I don't know how I got there or what happened to me. Obviously I got out but I don't remember a thing. The anchors show the footage of the cloud of dust. I walk to the bathroom and look in the mirror. I'm coated in the stuff. So is the windowsill outside, like the courthouses were. They say it'll take weeks to clear. It takes me half an hour and twenty-five paper towels to clean myself off. There's another set of clothes hanging on the back of the bathroom door—they fit. Of course. This is my office. What else could it be?

I head back to the desk and sit. I turn off the TV. I pull the wallet out of my pocket. The picture on the driver's license looks something like me. Why shouldn't it? The address is in Staten

Island. I couldn't get there anyway—the ferry's not running. Or do I have a car? I call 411 to get my own phone number. The phone rings a long time. No answer, no machine, but no one picks up either.

I should just go home. I should get a cab. There have to be cabs running. I'd have to walk above 14th Street—they aren't letting anyone downtown. But I could get a car to the address. I have lots of keys. Something will fit. Why do I doubt this? Why don't I feel anything for the address? Why do I doubt that I will know it either when I get home?

Because everything is strange. I acknowledge the overview, the world I live in, but everything has changed simply because familiarity has disappeared. I'm not talking about familiarity with something in particular—the whole *concept* of familiarity is gone. Everything is at a distance, removed, detached from me, from any associations, from feeling or pleasure or dread or pain. Pain floats over the city in a cloud. It takes no effort to identify. But you can't touch a cloud. It communicates nothing. It offers nothing on its own. It's just there.

Just as I'm about to feel something—just as the fear and fright begin to become palpable—there's a knock at the door. I left it hanging when I came in, so all she has to do is push on it to get it open.

"I need help," she says, sitting in the chair across from me. "I'm trying to find a missing person."

"Aren't we all?" I answer.

Bridge and Tunnel People

March 31, 2003

"Bridge and Tunnel people."

"What is this?"

"This is what they call us—bridge and tunnel people, like everyone should be able to afford Manhattan."

"It's status," S replied. "The Manhattan people look down on the Queens people, the blacks think the Jews are cheap, the Irish think the blacks are lazy, the hip-hoppers think the punk people are not hip, anybody making over $100,000 a year hates the Democrats, and someday the Natives are going to hate the guys who put up the casinos for taking all their money."

"We won't live to see that one," said M.

"Thanks be. But I see it every day in the store. They all come in talking about everybody else, like nobody knows as good as them. And like I'm not there at all."

"That's because you're bridge and tunnel people. Nobody sees us anyplace. We're below everybody."

"Take the upper level or the bottom?"

"The top makes better pictures. Don't you pay attention?"

"This is not about me," S replied. "Things will happen according to plan, despite my weakness."

"Where do you get this nonsense? You watch Oprah too much."

"It's a good show. She at least helps people sometimes. Did you leave food for the dogs?"

"Lots of food," M assured him.

"The ones from the Towers, they sent out people to their houses to save their dogs. We should have that," S said.

"Are you comparing yourself?"

"No, no, it's the dogs I'm thinking of."

The line of cars was stacked up along the approach ramp. Two trucks were moving slowly in adjoining lanes, which held up everyone behind them.

"This is rudeness," S said. "They know people are in a hurry."

"Yeah—this is New York. Everybody has very important travel plans," his passenger echoed and they both laughed. "Watch the pothole."

"No problem at this speed," S assured him. He was able to steer around it in any case. The van lumbered carrying the weight in the back but he had practiced for a week with sandbags and cinder blocks to simulate it and the handling was pretty much what he expected.

"I saw two American girls in the neighborhood wearing burkas," S said. "You think this means something?"

"They'll be wearing them with miniskirts this summer," M answered. "They take nothing seriously."

"Nothing?"

"They fight a war on terrorism and on the front page of the newspaper for weeks is 'Joe Millionaire.'"

"That won't change, you don't think?" S asked. M heard the twinge in his voice and recognized a destructive sort of doubt seeping into his driver's resolve. This could not go unanswered.

"I think over time, things must change," he said. He could see S considering him between glances at the traffic, which was further snarled by an accident ahead. "When people are comfortable, they want to stay comfortable. When all the real choices are uncomfortable, they watch television instead. They have to be made uncomfortable so that their minds adjust. Then making a choice becomes a necessity."

S seemed to be considering this, considering it at greater length than M liked.

"How do we know they'll make the right choice?" he asked.

M stifled the temptation—it was strong in him—to squash this altogether. This is the wrong question, he thought, but did not say.

"It is not for us to know the results of our work. The world goes the way the world goes," he added, thinking this might appeal to S's Oprah-watching side. "All we can know is our role." He smiled. "We're bridge and tunnel people, that's our role."

S laughed, and the tension eased. They passed the accident and now they were climbing the ramp with a small group of cars, heading for the tall bridge towers and the broad roadway over the river. The sun came from behind a cloud and gleamed on the stanchions.

"Look at the new Mercedes," S said, always watching the machines. He wasn't good for much but he knew his machines.

"Yeah—see the look he's giving us," M added.

"Bridge and tunnel, that's what he's saying," S said. "We're almost there."

"Roll down the window," M suggested, climbing into the back of the van. "Tell him if there's no bridge, there's no bridge and tunnel people."

He mouthed a prayer and bent to push the red button.

The Lawyer's Story

February 20, 2003

I used to be a matrimonial attorney. You think it's all guys who've beaten up their women and they come in with sunglasses to cover the bruises, the bums. But we also had a gold digger club.

I had one woman who came in—hot little number. She's around 40, he's 68. He's a bum, she says, he cheated on me, I want everything he's got. We hire a detective—he's an off-duty cop, he gets a couple hundred a week to follow people for us, take pictures, you know, the usual kind of thing. So he follows the old guy around. He walks stooped over he's got his lunch in a paper bag, you can see the apple at the bottom of the bag yknow. So after a couple of days, we have the detective follow her. She comes out of a health club in Bay Ridge, kind of a ritzy place, you know and she's coming out with the personal trainer, who's like a Fabio type with dark hair and he's got one hand on her tit and the other down her back pocket. And our guy gets the picture.

So I ask her to come by my office and she's like Oh I'm kind of busy and I say it's important. So she comes by and I leave the one photo on the desk in an envelope and I tell her I have to go to the bathroom, being an old guy—I'm 61—would you please just have a look at this while I'm gone and tell me what you think. You know, I don't' have to rub it in, right?

So I come back, her whole jaw is on the table, she's like "Ohhh." I say, "Now look, I don't sit in judgment, that's not my job. But if we're going to court, it's a war and if you take the bullets out of my gun, we get killed. So I need to know what's coming—is there anyone else?" She finally says, "One other." So of course, since we caught her lying already and she's admitting to one other, there's probably a few more someplace. So I ask her, "What do you want?" And she, without a second's hesitation, says, "$15,000 a month, the primary residence, the Mercedes and sole custody of the kids." I tell her "Well, I will go to the other side and talk to them, but I think that's unlikely. But I'll try."

So I call the other lawyer, he says 'Come down tomorrow at 10.' I get to his office and he says, "Okay, here is what I will propose and what your client will accept. $60,000 a year, the primary residence, a car—unspecified, and sole custody with liberal visitation." Then he looks at me and he says, "Tell your client that, between the waist and the knees, she's not the best and not the worst, but she's way too liberal about the entry fee. It's been nice talking at you—welcome to the big leagues." He was a tough guy, this lawyer.

So I went back and gave her the offer. I didn't tell her what he said, cause how could I? This didn't seem to get through. She said, "That's a third of what I wanted." I said, "Okay, but look at this way: You're getting $60,000, the house paid for, the car paid for, you're getting 25% of his income for child support and you work two days a week. So you're going to end up with about $100,000 a year. The other thing to remember is: they've got detectives just like we do. My advice is: take the deal." It took her five days but she took it.

Every once in a while, the shoe is on the other foot. One guy, I was representing his wife, he called me and said, "Can I come down and talk to you?" I said I can't do that, it's against the Code of Ethics. So he shows up at the office and plants himself in the door and says, "Let's just go to lunch. Just eat with me." So I go like an idiot. And he says, "This is going to cost me a lot of money." I say, "Well, that's what you have a lawyer for. You can fight it and maybe bring it down a little, but you should find a way to make it work for the both of you." He was in the waste management business, you know? One of those guys. So he had a 42 year old wife who he's dumped for a 40 year old number a little hotter than the wife and he wants out. But he repeats, "This is gonna cost me a lot of money." And then he says, "I think maybe I should get somebody to bump her off." And I knew I was in trouble then, so I told him, "Look—I've got an account here, but we've got to leave now because I can't hear this, and I have to report it, understand?"

So we left and I went back to the office and we dropped her as a client, because now I had guilty knowledge of both of them, and I called the District Attorney. I told him what the guy said and he said "Oh shit—why were you having lunch with this guy?" and I said "He planted himself in the office and wouldn't take no." So they dragged him in and he said he had a little wine—he only had a Diet Coke, but I wasn't going to contradict him—and just got loose and said things he shouldn't have but he didn't mean it. And he got off on it. But the DA turned him over to the IRS, who discovered he hadn't paid his taxes in nine years. I saw him a year later and he comes up to me and I thought, O God, he's going to deck me but he puts his arms around me and says Pallie, I should have listened to you and settled, I should've taken your advice. The IRS got me and she took me to the cleaners and the girlfriend doesn't want me anymore. I should have listened to you. And I thought, this is what got me a heart attack—caring too much.

A Shiver and a Crack

March 29, 2009

Mark and Susan met at Danny's on Saturday morning, five days after September 11th. There were several customers waiting for booths to free up for breakfast when Mark said, "Why don't we just eat together?" He and Danny pulled a couple of tables together in the back room, the walls mounted with pictures of zebras and rhinos, baboons and elephants Danny's son had taken on vacation two years earlier, in the peaceful years following the end of history.

Pam and Tom joined them but neither talked a whole lot. Pam had lost her husband aboard one of the jets that crashed into the Towers. Tom wasn't her husband but he had the same name as her husband and he'd already moved in with her. All of this information was readily available from Danny's waitresses,

Consuela and Lucy, who knew everything about everyone, all over the world, just ask.

With the other two not talking much, Mark tried amiably to fill the gap, bringing up the weather—it had turned colder the previous day. That topic died, without much effort to preserve it. Susan responded with a comment about Bob Dylan's new album, which he hadn't heard. After a few more dead ends and fleeting attempts at comments by Pam—Tom just smiled and listened to the others—Mark said, "Did you hear about the hijacker? The one who actually lived in this neighborhood?"

Susan smiled a tortured smile. "He lived in my basement, actually," she answered.

She felt a grim satisfaction from the sudden intake of breath around the table—it's the way she'd been feeling the whole week. Pam went even whiter than usual and seemed entirely unable to speak. Susan felt sorry for her in particular. If there had been another way to answer—or a way not to answer—Susan would have taken it. But there wasn't, not really, not for her. What Susan felt, she would say, eventually, inevitably. She was a creature of limited control. It was just the way she was.

"When was this?" Mark asked, actually sounding a bit out of breath.

"About a year ago—that's when he left. He lived in the house about a year. He really didn't talk much—that's always what people say, isn't it? Serial killers, child molesters, the neighbors always say 'Such a quiet person, kept to himself.' That's how he was. I could hear him praying sometimes—he prayed a lot more at the end. He gave me just a couple of days notice moving out but he wasn't the first to do that." She was looking at the food on the table, her half-eaten egg, the yellow running across the plate under the home fries and those little round sausages Danny liked. "He liked motorcycles. Remember Bill Truitt, the guy with the handlebar mustache, was always in here? Worked for the Bridge and Tunnel? He had a Harley and...well, they'd always be talking out on the street about the bike. But he'd never take a ride—Bill offered him a couple times that I saw. He was afraid to ride on the back of the bike."

"But he flew a plane," Mark offered and she nodded. Pam winced and the conversation drifted immediately in other directions. When they'd all finished eating, Mark insisted on paying. "Just this once," he said. "I instigated so it's my party." When they stepped outside, the clouds parted just enough to let a few rays of sunlight through and the waitresses said they walked away together.

There were lots of people on the street despite the weather gone cloudy and gray. They were milling at the window displays and clustered around the park fence near the playground, talking and greeting each other, seeking company. Mark and Susan walked the long avenue next to each other without acknowledging in any way that they were together. But they already were, somehow. The decision not to separate was an unusual one for them and they were both very aware of it.

"The sun's trying to break through," Mark said finally.

"*Optimist*," she sneered.

"What's wrong with that?"

"Nothing wrong," she said. "You're just more courageous than me. I don't want to be disappointed so I always expect the worst."

He smiled at that. "I figure if I can't imagine something good, it can't happen. That doesn't mean I *expect* it."

She was running her hands through her the streaks of gray in her hair, he noticed, self-conscious maybe, but also playing with it, flirtatious. That was a sign, he knew, he remembered, a sign she was interested. He would have jumped on this when he was younger, he knew, fastened on it, gotten all lathered up about it. He'd have fashioned ten wild fantasies in three seconds out of that falling hair. Was she aware of it, of his noticing? Were women ever *not* aware of men noticing? Even if they *weren't* interested?

They walked two more blocks without speaking. He was aware of feeling relaxed, of not feeling the need to say anything. He was aware of that but not more than aware, not self-conscious himself. That was surprising, it was unusual for the last few years. He hadn't relaxed in an attractive woman's company in a while. Then again, he hadn't been in an attractive woman's company in a while either.

He found himself watching what she was watching, taking note of the things she paid attention to. She didn't seem much interested in clothes in the store windows but she did stop a few times to glance at fabrics, sashes on chairs and curtains ruffling the corners of store displays. People's faces passing—he was used to staring discreetly, fixing an image of someone in just a momentary glance and he noticed she seemed as aware of the striking faces as he was. And then, as they approached President Street, they both stopped spontaneously, independent of one another, to stare at a painting in a window. It was representational, just an interior of a back yard garden with sunlight cutting through at an angle. It appeared simple, almost naïve, at first, the surfaces barely modeled, the shadows almost opaque. But the coloring was superb and the whole effect somehow touching, almost heartbreaking. He stared at it for almost a minute before he noticed her face, the look she was giving it.

"You want it," he said.

"No—uh, well, who knows how much it is?" she answered.

"Tell you what—let's share it," he said. "Split the cost, you get custody for a month, then me."

She looked at him for a several seconds, the smile growing across her face despite her attempts to suppress it. "What a really horrible idea," she marveled and then they broke up laughing.

"Okay—I'll race you for it," he said. "Whoever gets inside and offers the guy the price first. But then we can't haggle him down. He'll play us against each other."

"But I don't want it," she said.

"Oh please," he said. "You're a terrible liar. It's all over your face."

"I get it the first month," she said and they went inside.

He carried it to her house and went in to help her hang it. She removed a Mary Cassatt print over the fireplace in her living room and placed it carefully in the closet. "It'll come back out in a month," she said as he hung the new painting. "This is the first real painting I've ever owned." She looked at him for a reply.

"I've been buying originals for a few years," Mark said a little sheepishly. "I saw a painting in a gallery window, just like we did here and I didn't buy it. I went home and dreamed about the thing for two nights in a row—that was it for me. I knew this one would stick with me too."

"I guess I've had those too," Susan mused, "but it never occurred to me to buy them."

"So I'll be a bad influence on you," he shrugged. "You won't be the first."

She smiled. "Any particular style you buy?"

"Cheap," he answered, laughing and she laughed too despite her reserve, both the reserve she maintained with men and the reserve she maintained against her own feelings. A look passed across her face nonetheless, a kind of grateful surprise at his humor. He recognized that look and the heat behind it and then followed a moment of real confusion, the two of them grappling with the obvious attraction between them that had become too obvious to ignore. "Listen," he offered, "I'd like to buy you dinner if you're interested."

She looked out the window, surprised to see the sun nestling near the horizon across the river. She felt her cheeks redden. "I...I can't," she stammered. "I can't date." He colored too and she felt terrible. She was trying to figure out how to explain what she meant as he backed toward the door, offering unnecessary apologies and let himself out. How old do I have to be, dammit, before I get these things right? She had just enough time to really regret her actions before she heard knocking just where he'd left.

Mark stood smiling like he'd just wandered by. "You're right, now that I think about it," he said. "I've been on so many horrible dates lately. It just *doesn't* work, does it?"

"No," she rushed to agree, to make sure he understood that this was what she meant, that she hadn't meant to throw him out. She was surprised and shaken about how happy she was to see him.

"I mean, I go to dinner and sit there trying to figure out how to be charming and attractive. Which is what I did when I was twenty. And the only problem is, I'm too old for that now. I know better. If I just genuinely have a good time, I'll be plenty charming and attractive. I just want somebody to like me the way I am anyhow. But that's not what a date is about, is it?"

"No, it's not," she said, a little breathless over his explanation.

"So, you're right, no date. I'm not buying dinner under any circumstances. What if we cooked something together some night? Would that be okay?"

"That would be very nice," she said, feeling her cheeks flush again and not caring a bit.

"Okay," he said, breathing as though filling his lungs after a climb. "So we just have to figure out what night." His eyes were bright, a young man's hungry eyes. On her. It had been a long time since she'd made a man that hungry. She basked in those eyes.

"Well," she said, making the decision in the middle of the sentence, "we have to eat tonight, don't we?"

He nodded. "That's what I was thinking." He was trying to remain low-key, to make it all very nonchalant. When she was younger, this would have made him seem disreputable somehow. Now, it just seemed futile and kind of cute—and hopeless. Maybe it was cute because she could see that he knew it was hopeless as well. "So—can I come in?" he said finally, having stood in the doorway awkwardly through this four-second simultaneous epiphany. She laughed and let him in and everything changed, because they both knew at that moment how the evening was going to play out.

He took her direction in the kitchen gracefully and was reasonably good—but not too good—with the tasks he was assigned. They were passing back and forth in close quarters, bumping into each other at first and then exchanging more purposeful touches as time went on. Mark in the middle of cutting carrots became very aware of the smile on his face, that it kept igniting all by itself, igniting out of nothing. Glancing sheepishly in her direction, he realized she was doing the same and a warm current immediately started at his fingers and toes and spread all through his body like dye in cotton. He felt like cotton suddenly, like he was made of cotton—light and airy, the breeze passing right through him. Lightheaded. They were talking to each other constantly but none of it sounded like anything—just words, assurances, I'm still here and so are you, we're here together. None of it meant anything as words but the message was outside the words—you don't feel this all alone, I'm with you, we're having this moment together. Both of them were wrapped up in the feeling of the moment, willing to wallow in it—but neither expected anything more than the evening. If you'd asked, neither would be sure they wanted anything more. Too complicated. Too much to deal with. Have my life the way I want it. I'm too hard to live with. I don't want to compromise.

But, just after dumping the chopped vegetables into the sauce, he turned and put his arm around her waist and she turned as though she'd been waiting for him. The kiss was more than they'd been expecting, though they'd been anticipating it every moment since he returned to the door. It led immediately to a kind of adult groping, skipping the intermediate steps and proceeding immediately to the pleasure zones. She was stunned at what she was letting him do and even more by what she was doing herself—she'd never gone after a man the way she did now. His touch was electric—he wasn't the first to have that effect on her but this was different simply because she'd taken for granted long before that she'd never feel that way again. The way he looked at her was a wonder—she remembered men looking at her that way but that memory came to her through more recent memories of men looking through her and past her, the vivid miserable experience of being invisible. She was thrilled to be exciting again and she was not foolish enough to think that she would have many more such opportunities.

Eventually, he leaned over her and flicked off the burners. "Later," he said and she led him into the bedroom.

The lovemaking was new for both of them. He hadn't been with a woman in over a year and was thrilled to find that everything still worked. But she was thrilled because he was slow and sensitive, focused on her pleasure instead of his own, intent on making her shiver and shake and lose control. Once he succeeded, she was determined to return the compliment and she took him with a hunger she didn't know she had, a hunger she'd never felt for her husband. She wondered if that was his fault or hers but she was too busy and happy to wonder for long.

They returned to the kitchen eventually to finish cooking dinner. She was wearing a pajama top and he the bottoms—he didn't ask whose they'd been originally. Once everything else was cooking, she mentioned she needed pasta. When he didn't react, she said, "It's downstairs." This didn't throw him either so she stood a while in the doorway until he turned to look at her—he still had that magical look on his face—and added, "Can you come with me?"

They went down the narrow staircase. It wasn't until they were down to the bottom floor and she'd slowed to a crawl, feeling in the dark for the light switch and then moving uncomfortably between the cardboard boxes marked with pre-printed labels 'Property of the United States of America' and her own food stores on countertops and shelves that he understood what she'd meant, what this place was.

She shrugged at the first box. "They took all the stuff that was actually relevant to the...case," she said. "At least they said they did. They said they'd come back for this but, in the meantime, I'm doing storage for the Federal Government."

"They won't let you move it?"

"Who do I ask?" she said.

"Well, who's in charge? The FBI?"

"When they come," she said, "they come in a group with badges and they don't tell you who's in charge." She looked at the boxes. "They wanted to know why he'd left so much stuff behind. He said he was going to come back for it too. And then I got used to not locking up down here so I didn't hurry to find someone else." She found the pasta and turned for the stairs again.

"Did they think you were helping him?"

"They didn't think I was a terrorist, I don't think," she said. Then she squirmed, shrugging her shoulders. "They wanted to know if I was having an affair with him." She responded to Mark's look by mewling, "He was a *baby*." She started as soon as the words came out. "That's not what I mean," she said immediately. "Jesus! I don't mean a baby…not with what he did…he wasn't…I don't know…" She fizzled out, helpless, looking to Mark for help.

"You knew him as a *person*," he offered, sounding as helpless as she had.

"But I *didn't*," she moaned like an animal. "He wasn't a person—he was a *tenant*." A nervous laughter bubbled up out of her; she wrapped her arms around herself. "He was the guy who rented the basement—not even the basement, the front rooms in the basement—I locked the door to the staircase so I could keep the back for myself, so I could have the garden. He paid the rent the first of the month, cash, he didn't play music loud, he didn't have parties so I was happy. I heard him praying once in a while and it sounded romantic. I had a Muslim downstairs. I congratulated myself for being so cosmopolitan." The laughter choked off, reduced to a nasty gargle.

"Enough," he said. He didn't want to see this, didn't want to watch her come apart. "He's dead." She paused for a moment but it was merely a pause, a catching of breath, so he pressed on. "He lived here, fine. He was a tenant. There's no reason for you ever to have thought of him in any other way. He lived here, he didn't give you trouble, he moved out. That's enough. You don't have to think any more about it than that."

"How?" she asked. "How do I stop?"

He switched off the light and they went upstairs to finish cooking. After dinner, he said, "Do you want to get out of here? Come to my place overnight?" He was expecting a quick 'no' — when he didn't get it, he went awkward. "It's...it's a bachelor's place. I've gotten used to being alone so everything is right where I put it down last. It might be disgusting, I have no idea."

"You don't have to offer," she said and he recognized this immediately as a 'yes.'

"I'd love it if you wanted to—I'll promise to clean up later."

"I can help," she offered.

He made breakfast in bed the next morning. She seemed comfortable reading the paper that morning but, when it got to afternoon, she said "My place is nicer."

"No doubt," he admitted.

"The kitchen is bigger too."

"True."

"Why don't we have dinner at my place again?"

Crossings

April 17, 2007

I could see his eyes—his pupils—six blocks away.

The light had gone green and the cars were scrambling and spreading out, hunting for position. As I pulled to the left, there he was, perched on the center divider, in a parka and checkered woolen hat, stocky and slightly comical. There's someone on the divider every day—in Brooklyn, crossing at the crosswalk is for wimps and people who have time and no one has time. But he could easily have crossed before we reached him and I found myself wondering why he was waiting. No one, as I said, has time in Brooklyn. Except him. This guy had loads of time.

I had been jockeying the last ten blocks with a black Mazda. The guy kept cutting me off but as soon as he got in front of me, he would slow down. He didn't want to go anyplace; he just wanted to be first. Now I'd finally got ahead of him and was putting some space between us—I don't want to fuss on the way to work, I just want to get there. And all at once I see this face on the divider staring at me, staring so I can see his eyes clear as a bell six blocks away and somehow all I could wonder was why he hadn't crossed the street already.

The cop asked me later, "Did you get any warning?" and I said "No" but it felt like a lie immediately and I stammered, "Well, it seemed like he was looking at me."

"What do you mean, looking at you?" He stopped scribbling in his pad. He had one of those big loose-leaf pads, not the real big college ones but one that was too big to fit in any pocket but a cop's.

"Like he was looking right at me, like he could see my face, while I was coming. I mean, the second before he jumped, I already had my foot off the gas, just for a second, like I knew he was going to." *Because I saw something in his eyes. Because I could read everything that would happen in his eyes.*

"And—?" The cop's eyes narrowed. He was younger than me and he'd probably seen plenty in his—what? ten years on the force maybe? The look on his face craved simplicity, an answer he could file on his way to lunch and then home to the kids.

"Nothing," I shook my head. "It didn't matter. I hit the brake as soon as I saw him jump but it was too late."

The cop nodded. "Could see that from the tire tracks," he murmured. He was watching me closely though. "Did you know him?" he asked, eyes tight on me.

"No," I shook my head. "Never saw him before," and as I said it, I felt my face screw up like I'd smelled something bad. I couldn't be proud of that expression—the guy was dead, after all. But he jumped, so I didn't see any reason I should have to get too reverent about him either. The cop considered this a moment longer, before putting the pencil in his pocket and closing his notebook.

"Just stay put a minute, in case somebody else wants to talk to you," he said.

"I'm not going anywhere."

I waited while he walked off to join the other cops down by the curb, where EMS had just arrived, the whole wolf pack surrounded by rubberneckers crowding the yellow tape. All of us—the cops, me, EMS, dead body—huddled at a gas station right where it happened. Somebody brought me a cup of coffee from the station café—I have no idea who. I don't drink coffee but I drank this. I couldn't taste it anyway. They slid a body bag around the guy but then they had a hard time lifting it into the back of the van. The weight kept shifting like it was moving around on its own.

How many other people had gone by? Before he jumped, that is. He was already on the divider when I first saw him. I'd assumed he'd finished crossing the westbound side of the street and was just waiting to go the other half. But what if he hadn't? What if he'd been standing there for ten minutes—or an hour—waiting?

Waiting for what?

EMS pulled away and most of the people at the yellow tape took off, to work or vandalism or whatever else they did to while away the time. The few that were left were now looking at me. I guess I was more interesting than the cops, who saw this kind of stuff every day and were all involved with their spiral notebooks, getting their stories straight in case there was a lawsuit or something. They kept staring at me, the people at the tape, staring like I didn't see them staring, like their eyes would bounce right off me, like I didn't notice or didn't care or wouldn't feel anything if I did. All of them but one. She was a woman around my age, short and bulky with Inuit eyes. She stared like the others but when I stared back, she turned away, pierced, and I thought, this one's got a heart at least.

Finally the cops started climbing back into their cars. The detective in charge gave me his card, said he'd be in touch if there were any other questions. The mechanic said my car was okay to drive to the body shop—I saw he'd washed most of the blood off the fender.

The gas station owner was eyeing me like I should at least fill up or something before I was on my way, here's your hat what's your hurry? His eyes bounced off mine, like the others. I had no story for him. The Inuit woman didn't know my story, but she knew I had one. I'd seen that flash of recognition in her eyes, in the instant before she turned away.

Just like the man on the divider. My eyes hadn't bounced off his, hadn't gone blank or evaded his stare, even when I sensed what was coming, even in that instant when I lifted my foot off the gas.

He'd been standing there forever in the morning chill, his feet gripping the concrete edge, waiting for a sign, for the signal to trigger his last step. He didn't even know what he was waiting for until he found it in my eyes.

Like I told the cop, I'd never seen him before.

But now I'd see him forever.

Red Sky

March 14, 2009

Revised: March 15, 2021

In the afternoon, as the awful red-brown smudge spread across the harbor, they stood and watched the exodus, the endless, aimless procession of the hollow-eyed, the victims, the witnesses, walking home, walking toward home, just walking.

First had come the shower, just after the towers collapsed — paper, bits of cloth, that awful whitish ash, fluttering down out of the sky, like manna from heaven — except manna was deliverance and this was dread. Pam watched the debris drifting onto the neat gardens and windowsills. The first sight of that whitish coating sent a chill up into her shoulders and it wouldn't go away.

If the weight of the world's problems fell on Manhattan, it was only fitting. Manhattan thrived on tumult, on pressure and notoriety. Brooklyn had always felt just separate enough, a healthy distance. But not anymore. First, the refuse of the world's troubles drifted out of Manhattan's skies, onto Pam's stoop, the flower boxes and the tiny patch of lawn Tom trimmed every weekend in spring and summer. And now, an hour later, the first groups of the lost and frightened and shell-shocked, marching through Park Slope, seeking distance, that distance that might never come again.

Sheila was with Pam in the kitchen having coffee when the news broke on the TV. "Didn't I tell you I heard something?" Sheila said, going to the back window, proud of herself for a moment. And then both their faces changed when the news reader announced the plane had come from Boston.

"It's not his flight," were the first words out of Pam's mouth. He would have called. Regardless of anything, he would have called. "And he's going to Los Angeles," she continued.

Surely it was all a mistake anyway. A bomber had flown into the Empire State Building once, years ago. So now it had happened again. Although, the news readers cautioned, that earlier incident had taken place in a fog. The words echoed in Pam's head; when she stepped to the window and looked out through the clear blue sky, her stomach growled. Sirens howled across the river.

It was ten minutes before they started up the stairs to the roof. The premonition was in them both and, maybe for that reason, they just resisted moving. They arrived at the rail just in time to see the second plane hit. And then, there was a long time when the world seemed filtered through a haze. The billowing smoke seemed as if it should have made a tremendous noise but neither of them remembered hearing one. There was no sound now other than the sirens that never ended, that multiplied, whining from every direction, like car alarms after an earthquake.

First, traffic stopped on the highway and then the local streets snarled, the whole neighborhood drawn to a standstill, watching the spectacle, unable to move. From the roof, the chatter, voices and whispers, drifted up from the street—Pam absorbed bits and pieces as she nursed the dregs of her coffee. A plane had attacked the Pentagon. Another was on its way to attack the White House—no, the Capitol. And then it just didn't happen—no word about why. Other planes were still on the way, the voices said, though the skies were now eerily clear.

Just words, words and more words. And then, clearly, inevitably, so clear she could replay the timbre of the voice, the inflection of the words, in her head forever after: the first plane was Boston-to-LA; they chose it because of all the jet fuel, all that fuel *to burn*.

She turned and saw the look on Sheila's face, that she'd heard it too. But it wasn't conclusive…there were other flights from Boston to LA. Nobody had called from the company or his clients…

She went down into the house for her cell and dialed and got no answer. The call went to voice mail and she heard his voice saying 'You know what to do' but she couldn't bring herself to do anything, even though her lips moved and she pressured the back of her throat, trying to coax sound into the air. Sheila refilled the coffee and paced, fretting over who to call but Pam drifted away, away through the rooms overlooking the street, somehow light and free and untouched. The walls of her house were bright as always, sunlight bouncing through the lace curtains, the light sharp, blooming, like the ball of fire cutting through the smoke when the second plane hit. Was that the plane from Boston? Or, which one was for LA, if they were both from Boston?

Tom didn't want white walls, he kept talking about repainting but they couldn't decide on a color and she liked the idea of *adding* color with furnishings instead. Sheila said there had to be a list somewhere of the passengers but Pam was still drifting, up the stairs again and onto the roof. Sheila caught up with her just in time for the first tower going down. After that, they just waited, knowing, both of them, silent for twenty minutes until the second one fell. The coffee was cold by then—Pam hadn't drunk a drop, just kept stirring idly with her finger.

They heard the cries this time—not only the neighbors, but across the river. The hole in the skyline registered instantly in Pam as a conclusion. *Game, set and match.* Now she could go downstairs and sit at the kitchen table, stirring a fresh cup of coffee, without any expectations. She didn't try to call anyone and she didn't expect the phone to ring.

Sheila lured her out to the stoop later, saying she wanted a smoke. "It's not a bar," Pam said. "You can smoke inside."

"I don't want to stink up the place," Sheila replied. Pam could feel her watching, waiting for the emotional reaction that, surely, had to come. Pam was waiting for it herself. She knew what had happened—she'd seen it, for God's sake. She could hear her own voice, in the back of her head, repeating details she didn't quite comprehend, over and over.

Neighbors she knew, people she'd seen on the block for years, taking out the garbage, staring out the window, coming home from the supermarket—were out in the street now, talking, chattering like birds, embracing. Mrs. Colletti next door called to her from the wheelchair on her ramp by the kitchen; Pam flexed a little smile and offered a wave, a ridiculous little wave, almost the Queen Mother wave. How long had they lived next door to each other without a substantial conversation? A moment later, Sheila was there, speaking to the old woman, who went silent, almost shame-faced. When Sheila returned, Pam asked her to just let people talk from then on.

It was Tom's plane. That was the voice in her head, the words echoing like a foreign language—the gist was clear but none of the words had force. The outside world wasn't synching up yet with the one inside.

As morning drifted into afternoon, it began to remind her of the Marathon. The pilgrimage escaping Manhattan this day mirrored the progression of the Marathon runners—the first group determined, brisk and efficient, the next dogged, adhering to some obscure internal clock and the rest trudging forward in resignation, just hoping to reach the end of the race. Here and there, she heard angry voices, specifying culprits and villains; but mostly, they were silent and shell-shocked; pall bearers who hadn't recognized the corpse.

It got darker. Pam found herself climbing to the roof again. The floodlights at the site in Manhattan weren't bright enough to drown out the raging fire.

A light went on next door and she watched Mrs. Colletti wheel herself into her bedroom and lift herself carefully onto the edge of the bed. Ten minutes of preparations followed—pushing the wheelchair into the corner, removing makeup and pins from her hair, carefully, meticulously. Pam felt a tear rolling down her cheek without being aware of any conscious reason. Sheila returned, guided Pam down the stairs and poured a couple of Scotches into her. Pam would have sworn she didn't feel the booze but the next thing she saw was morning light creeping through the curtains.

The television got a lot of mileage out of the thicket of flyers along Broadway, pleas for news of people who'd gone missing, who might have been in the towers or might have been in the subway or might have gone for breakfast somewhere or might just have run late. There were so many 'lucky' stories, too—*I broke the heel on my shoe so I was ten minutes late and now I'm alive!*

She watched and watched, waiting to crack. Eventually, she had to, didn't she? She knew what she'd seen. But it wasn't real. Tom dead wasn't real. She wondered if Tom alive had ever been real.

'You lack feeling,' Tom said.

'It's there,' she'd answered, 'I just keep it to myself.'

'What good is it if you don't share it?' His last words, on his way out the door. *I remember*, she thought, hugging herself, arms tight round. *I don't forget things, I just don't know what to do with them.*

Sheila called to say she was running some things over to her mother in Canarsie and would be back in half an hour or four, depending on traffic. No one seemed to know what to do with this day. It wasn't possible to go to work so everyone was saying stay home. More to the point, nothing you could think of doing felt right. Sheila was apologetic but Pam told her, *No rush on my account.*

She went outside with a bucket of water and a washcloth, to wipe the windowsills and clean the gunk off the flowers, though it quickly became clear that either the gunk would kill them or the cleaning would, those were the choices. Danny from the diner stopped by on his way to open—it must be earlier than Pam thought. He smiled and watched her through narrowed eyes as he asked her questions and listened, with extravagant sympathy, to her answers. Not that she knew what she was saying. All she knew was that Danny was hunting—already. Had word gotten around so soon? Danny was a known horndog, a player without limits.

Someone told her he'd installed a bedroom in the basement of the diner, so as not to waste opportunities. *Not with me*, she thought. She didn't think she'd said anything out loud but, when she looked up, Danny was turning to go.

She noticed the other man while watching Danny walk away. Tall but not standing tall, stooped and reticent in a way tall men rarely are. Watching her from across the street, though his eyes never quite focused on her.

Crossing the street, stopping in the sunlight to let a car pass, she saw the fresh scar on his forehead and the pale dust still in his hair, on his coat and shoes. He looked vaguely familiar but she wasn't sure she could recognize anyone at the moment. He was visibly fighting himself, eyes flickering back and forth, stepping in one direction and then another, a man on a mission but not quite sure what that mission was. He reached her gate in this hesitant fashion, grabbed onto the gatepost like a life raft and somehow, she didn't retreat into the house, though it was her first impulse.

Suddenly, his hand was reaching toward her, offering the wallet from his jacket pocket. "Is...this...?" he stammered.

His hand quivered. She had to focus to see what was in it—finally, she had to grab his wrist, to stop his wavering, to see it clear. It was Tom's driver's license, his picture and signature and his credit cards stacked above and behind and then the whole thing was in Pam's hand and inside was a slip of paper with notes about the bulbs he needed to order for the kitchen and an apology he'd started but never quite finished.

"Am...I...?" he started again and the look on the man's face was so hopeful and helpless and suddenly Pam reached out and pulled him inside the gate.

She enveloped him in a hug. She didn't realize it until he gently pulled away. "I'm...getting you all...dusty," he said and she looked down and saw the chalky stuff all over her blouse and jeans. The look on his face would swallow up an ocean, confusion and pain and hope all mingled. His eyes flickered to...her hand. The wallet was in her hand.

"Is...is that me?" he said finally and his voice, too, was overpacked, quaking, desperate. The emotion in it was naked, a tone of voice that didn't fit her ordered life.

And, at that moment, she stalled. Her heart stalled. Of course, she thought, he isn't Tom. Tom was on the plane. She saw the plane...or she saw the other one, whichever. He couldn't be Tom. He was on the ground and Tom...wasn't. Couldn't he see, in her face...that he wasn't? Surely something was missing on her face?

He didn't seem to notice a thing.

"Look at you!" she stammered, snapping up straight like a sergeant. "You're a mess! You need a shower and a change, don't you?"

He smiled, a tiny sheepish and totally uncomfortable smile. She pulled him up the steps and into the bathroom. He looked a bit lost. "You remember how to work it?" she said, pointing to the bright metal spike that rose from bath spigot to shower head.

"I...I can do it," he said and she closed the door behind her. She returned a few minutes later. "I'm leaving a change of clothes outside the door," she announced and went downstairs to make breakfast.

She made pancakes—everybody likes pancakes, she figured. When he came down from the shower, his shirt sleeves were too short and the pants hung low around his waist. He saw her staring and rolled up the sleeves, so on some level, he had to be aware they didn't fit. He stared at the stove, the curtains on the windows, the pancakes and at Pam, as though each was a concept he needed to translate from a foreign tongue. Then he sat down and tore into the first stack, putting away four or five in rapid succession before that addled, sheepish grin appeared on his face again and he relaxed into a more gradual pace.

"How do you take your coffee?" she asked.

"I..." he paused and concluded, "like yours." She realized how grateful she was for that open face of his. It wasn't the male gaze she was so used to, that hungry, expectant look she dreaded. She put the coffee on the table and sat opposite him.

"What do you remember?" she asked.

He slowed, gathering himself to the task of answering, of remembering. "Walking," he said. "My legs ached—that's the first thing I remember. I must have been walking a long time to get them like that but I don't remember it happening. I was by Times Square—"

"You remember Times Square? The name was familiar?"

"They told me where I was," he said.

"With the dust on you—"

He nodded. "I guess. Somebody from a bodega gave me a bottle of water but most people stayed away from me. It's scary...not remembering. You know you should recognize things, signs, names, you should be able to do something with them but somehow, you can't. I was afraid of streetlights at first or every time a car came around a corner, though the few cars were moving real slow. No one talked to me—it was like I was a ghost—and, every once in a while, I'd see myself in a window and then I knew it for sure.

"I slept behind a bush someplace. This morning, I remembered my wallet—I felt it in my jacket pocket. So, when the sun came up, I came here."

"The wallet was in your jacket pocket?"

"Uh-huh." It looked like Tom's suit. How did he get Tom's suit? Her mind was racing. He didn't say I came *home*, she thought. He said, I came *here*. He wasn't playing up to her. He wasn't pretending to know what he didn't. But he said *my* wallet. *That wallet,* she thought, *is the closest thing to a memory he has* and was relieved she hadn't taken it from him.

"I'm sorry for staring," he finished, shaking his head. "I'm sorry for not remembering."

It was an honest stare—he liked the look of her and he needed her. He wasn't pretending to a past he didn't know—he was just here in the moment and being open about it. She put her hand out across the table and laid it on his. They were smooth hands, not laborers hands. The fingers were long like an artist's.

The clock chimed on the wall over the oven--Sheila might arrive anytime now.

"We'll just have to start over, I guess," Pam said. "Maybe things will come back to you in time."

"I guess," he murmured.

What was wrong with her? His hand was warm. Tom's hands *never* felt warm. In the middle of summer, he was an oasis of cool. This wasn't Tom, she knew he wasn't Tom, Tom was dead in an airplane, an angel of death, an angel of someone else's vengeance out of the sky, manna from someone's vengeance out of the sky.

The words didn't work. Had they ever? How could words work when you could twist them any way you wanted?

"Do you want to take a walk?" she asked.

She turned without a thought away from the water and led him uphill. The coop was open—she bought some vegetables. "I'll make a soup," she said. "What sounds good? What do you like?"

His eyes got big and open as he considered this. "What kinds are there?"

"Of *soup*?" She was giggling. "You don't remember *soup*?" He flashed his shy smile—she was beginning to look for it—and shrugged, a quiver of the shoulders.

"I remember chowder," he said. "But I know there's more."

"Chowder? What kind of chowder?" she demanded.

It took a moment. "Fish!" he answered triumphantly.

"That's *it*? Of all the soups, *that's* the one you remember?" she hectored and felt ashamed as his face slumped. He was so happy to remember a kind, any kind. "I'm sorry," she dissolved, "it's just a funny choice."

I've got it wrong, she thought. He doesn't know he isn't Tom. He doesn't know *anything*. Whatever doesn't make sense—the shirtsleeves, not remembering soup—he thinks it's his fault and that's all he knows. He's Robinson Crusoe on the beach and I'm Friday. Or maybe vice-versa.

They walked up to Seventh Avenue, each lugging one of the co-op cloth shopping bags. The few businesses on the street that had opened were more muted than usual, no music playing and nobody really trying to sell anything. The shopkeepers were out by the doors, talking to passers-by, as though that was their job. Or maybe everyone just needed to talk.

"Ice cream!" she exclaimed, catching a sign. "You must remember ice cream."

"I like it," he said immediately but, clearly, the details of this, too, eluded him.

"Do you remember what it tastes like?"

He thought about this for a moment. "I remember how it feels eating it," he said. *Was he simple?* she wondered, *Or was this the hole inside, that he can't answer even a silly question without thinking it through.* Was he like that before...before this happened? What would I have thought of Tom, in this situation? Who would he have *been*, in this situation?

He flagged the last few blocks home, stumbling and beginning to wander, babbling random phrases to himself. She was relieved that Sheila hadn't returned.

She suggested dinner but he climbed the stairs to the bathroom. After twenty minutes, she knocked on the door and heard him awake on the seat. When he emerged, he seemed dazed and very aware of himself, all at once. When she steered him toward the bedroom, he turned stiff, resistant.

"This is an odd situation," she told him. "I'll take the guest room. You need the good bed to sleep. You need to sleep."

"Right now, I could sleep on the floor," he said and sunk onto the bed, snoring, to prove it before she could think of a reply.

Sheila showed up in the morning, just walked in the front door the way she was used to, as they were sitting down to breakfast. "Where were you yesterday?" she began. "I came by twice, left messages—" and then she stopped all at once, seeing the man at the table. Pam was up quickly, pulling her back out onto the stoop. "Who is he?"

"He's got Tom's wallet," Pam said, as though that explained anything.

"What?"

"He's got Tom's wallet. He showed up yesterday. He doesn't know who he is. He found the wallet and I guess he thinks maybe he's Tom."

"You *guess*?"

"He thinks he's Tom. He's not sure of things."

"Wait—okay but—what do you—?"

"He's *lost*," Pam said, "lost and alone. He needs help. His only hope is, he's Tom. Otherwise, he's got no memory, no past. Isn't that awful?"

"Pam, you can't do this!" Sheila said.

"What if Tom had…to go through this? What if he'd somehow been through this awful thing and come out on the other side…?"

"Pam!"

"That would change him, wouldn't it? It would have to!"

"Pam, this is crazy!"

"I'm *not* crazy! He's not Tom, I get that! I do, really! But if Tom was out there, in this situation, if he wandered into someone else's house and didn't know who he was—wouldn't we want him to get help?"

"From someone else's wife?"

"It's not like that," Pam said. "It's just until he remembers, until he's ready to go."

"What if he doesn't remember? What if he *stays*?" Sheila said. "How could he have Tom's wallet?"

"How do I know? They found one of the hijacker's wallets, didn't they?"

A truck rumbled by on the street—after the silence of the last few days, the roar was shocking. "*Why* are you doing this?" Sheila asked.

"Because I *can*," Pam said, her voice clear and certain. Clear and certain wasn't anything she felt.

But it seemed to sway Sheila, who smiled faintly and patted her shoulder. "What do you want me to do?" she asked.

"Just be my friend," Pam answered. "Just be yourself." She was about to go inside when Sheila stopped her.

"Do you want me to call him Tom?" she asked and Pam winced at the sound of it.

"You don't have to call him anything right now," she said.

He was poring over the paper, his forehead fretted and chin set. He wasn't getting far; he kept worrying the same section at the top of the page back and forth, trying to take it in.

"Do you remember anything?" Sheila asked. Pam shot her a dirty look, which she ignored but he didn't object.

"None of this," he said wonderingly, as though how could anyone not remember this and Pam thought *what a lucky man you are.*

He pulled the wallet from his pocket and held it in his hand, hefting and squeezing the leather. Pam watched and her face grew more alarmed as he continued.

Sheila grabbed her and dragged her back outside. "You *can't* do this," she told her, so loud that Pam's major concern became that he would hear. "What happens when he remembers?" she demanded. "How's he going to feel then? What do *you* get out of it?"

"Don't ask," Pam pleaded. "I don't know." She was wringing her hands until the knuckles turned white. "It's—it's something *good*."

"You think you can make something *good* out of this?" Sheila asked. "Now you're worrying me." She clapped her hands around Pam's temples. "Darling, you're in hiding."

"I'm *not*," Pam said firmly. "I have no one; he has no one. He's not aggressive; he's grateful. I'm helping him. He's helping me."

"He won't be grateful forever," Sheila said.

"There's no such thing as forever," Pam replied.

Sheila found an excuse to leave, less than an hour later. From her, that was a statement. *Normally, she wouldn't pass up the opportunity to pity me for at least the rest of the day,* Pam thought and immediately felt guilty for judging, for being clever at Sheila's expense. There were no perfect friends—Sheila was her friend.

When she went back inside, he was sitting at the computer, staring at the screensaver images of Ireland Tom had taken on their last trip together.

"Is this me or you?" he asked and she took a long moment to answer, "You."

She typed in the password and his desktop came up, with his hundred-and-fifty icons all over the screen. Pam's desktop had three. "You wholesale hoses, for vehicles. Cars and tractors and ships and…and airplanes, for that matter," she explained. "You used to have an office but now you do it from home."

"Hoses?" he smiled, a comical expression on his face. "Really?" And they shared a laugh that took her by surprise. It wasn't as if Tom had chosen the job anyway—it had just come along, like so many things in life. Just another thing that happened.

She went upstairs and opened the curtains and window shades, let the light into her bedroom, cracked the window to let in some air and lay down across the bed. After ten years of not smoking, she was dying for a cigarette.

With all the questions in her head, she fell asleep. When she woke, the sky was dull but the red light in the west still mingled with that muddy slash, that wound, across the harbor. Three days later, it was still there.

When she came down, he was bent over the coffee table. The wallet was out and he'd taken everything from it—the credit cards and the gym membership, Patrolmen's courtesy card and a fortune cookie explaining how to say 'tea' in Chinese. And a business card with Pam's birthday, her Social Security and cell number written on the back.

He was fingering them all, over and over, the way he'd fingered the wallet earlier. For what? Was he having doubts? She watched a moment longer and understood—he was just trying to make it real, the same way she was.

She sat on the couch next to him. "Who am I?" he asked, as though he'd rehearsed the question for a long while. She felt a chill up her back, but, really, how could that question be a surprise?

"You...are quiet," she began, "quiet a lot. You're deep—at least, I think you are. I'm more straightforward—I'm always cursing myself or congratulating myself for that." Her breath felt thicker, heavier, as she drew deeper down. "You've always withheld something from me, kept some part of yourself to yourself...not secret, really, I always could count on you being who you are but...but there are just things you don't talk about."

She looked to see how he was taking this. There was a poise in him now that she found unnerving, that hadn't been there, even just before she'd napped. He hadn't remembered everything—he couldn't have, surely?—but somehow, he didn't seem lost anymore either.

"You're really good at bolstering me, and needling me, knowing what I need. I'm tough on myself a lot but I didn't know I was until you told me." She caught her breath. She was breathing hard. He'd asked about himself but that wasn't the answer she was giving. She tried to yank herself back on track. "You're not your job. That's important to both of us. And I don't assume you'll like what I like. Somehow, that makes me feel secure—makes no sense, does it?"

He picked the driver's license off the table, holding it under the light and studying it for a moment before handing it to her. She hadn't really looked at it in a long time. The face staring back was not much like the one across the couch. Maybe hair color and the shape of the face—but the rest, the parts that gave character, were clearly not the same. She grew redfaced as he watched her compare the picture and his face.

It was *his* face now. He'd reclaimed it, found his own gaze, his own expression. At the gate, his expression had been a product of vacancy, evidence of something missing. That had changed.

"It's coming back?" she asked, a bit sad at losing him and sheepish at being left behind. "Your memory?"

He shook his head. "Not really," he said. "My name, my life—no, nothing. None of it." But his smile was relaxed, comfortable. "I like the story, the way you talk about—about me," he stammered for a moment. "It's the way I'd want someone to talk about me."

Pam was fading fast now, imagination running like a cart downhill. "No, uh…it's not fair, y'know, me telling you who you are," she stumbled. "I mean, that's what's so odd about people— you never really know who anybody is, do you?"

"Do you?" he asked.

"I don't know. It's just, I wouldn't want you to have to try to be who I told you to be. That wouldn't be right, would it? I want you to be who you are."

He smiled, that new smile of his. She found herself grateful to see it. It wasn't Tom's smile but it wasn't a bad smile either. "I'll try my best," he said.

Excerpt of 'Swindler & Son,' by Ted Krever

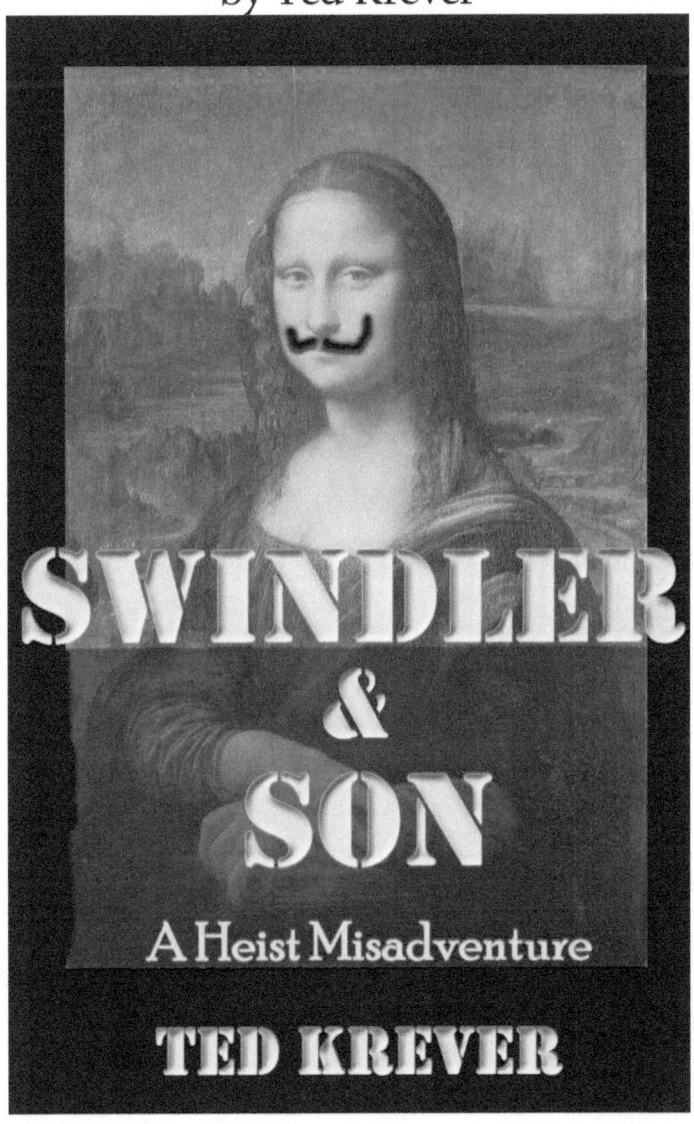

THE START

−So how does it start?

It starts with the sound of my own name spoken aloud.

Call me Nicholas, I'm fine. Nick or Nicky, even better.

But 'Nicholas Marsh' enunciated, first and last, all the way through—when I hear it *that* way, I know I've done something I'm about to pay for.

Hearing it in French, every syllable twisted and slurred and leaking from the earpiece of a Parisian counter-terrorism officer in a Kevlar vest, his back to me and his binoculars trained on my kitchen window—*that's* rock-bottom.

That's how it starts, in the snowy garden of the *Hopital Saint-Louis* in the Tenth Arrondissement, just past sundown on Christmas day, at what I fervently hoped was the end of one of the worst days of my life.

Well, actually, no...

Actually, it started about fifteen minutes earlier, on the other side of the canal, where I was mugged by some twenty-five year-old junkie in a purple-tinted mohawk and a leather jacket. And several nice tats on his neck that distracted my attention when I should have been focusing on his oncoming fist. He took my wallet and phone and left me aching and dizzy, which is why I wandered groggy several blocks out of my way and approached home through the garden.

I love that garden but none of the official exits land anywhere near my apartment. A few years ago, I found a back door, through the *Musee des Moulages* on the hospital grounds, that let me out near a construction gate right across the street from my building.

I'm just opening that back door when I hear my name and see GIGN, French Special Forces, two officers, huddled like Martians in flak suits, gas masks and sniper rifles, peeking through the construction gate at the wide corner, the entrance to my building and, eight floors above, at the dead coleus drooping from my night table.

Frozen in place, I scan the rooftops and find a squad of dark gray uniforms—and, in case I harbor any last doubts, hear my name one more time from the headset hanging from the blonde officer's right ear. I back instinctively into the doorway, sweating and making twenty-five different plans at the same time.

The bus! They won't be checking the bus on the Boulevard de la Villette, that's an answer. Having any sort of answer helps calms the quiver in my legs, brings them back into something like working order.

This is a mistake—it's got to be. If I'd done something to deserve counter-terrorism, I'd remember it, wouldn't I? More importantly, why in hell didn't somebody tip me off? Who do I know at GIGN?

Out through the door and the museum, retracing my steps, back out the far end of the compound, past the *Chapelle* to the *Rue de la Grange aux Belles*. Up toward the roundabout at a regular clip, walking briskly like a Parisian.

Am I thinking of escape? Hell no, I'm just getting pissed. Why hasn't somebody warned me? Why haven't they given me a chance to buy my way out of this?

Oh sure, GIGN makes it look serious but that just raises the price. I know somebody in every department of government and what they cost. Serious things have been undone before.

By the time the bus makes three stops, I know who to talk to—Beltoise, the second man at the *Surete*. He was at our Christmas party just last night.

I *own* him! At least, I should. If I had a middle-class clientele, if I dealt pot or owned a brothel, I could expect a phone call 24 hours in advance of a raid. It's common courtesy!

He'll be at *D'Azur*, of course, charging his dinner to us as usual.

When I arrive, he's tucked into a dim corner. He rises before I can reach him.

"Why is GIGN all around my apartment? You don't warn me?"

His eyes bulge like marbles. "Where's your phone?"

"Phone? Stolen. I got mugged."

He looks *relieved*. "That's why they're not here yet," he mutters and pulls me into the private room in back.

"Nicky, our past history—and the fact that I like you—is why I'll give you a minute's grace before I call you in." He's serious! His face goes cold—not like he doesn't know me, like he's never *seen* me before. "Normal corruption is one thing—but this?"

Normal corruption? Normal corruption is my *specialty*! He's reducing ten thousand years of civilized give-and-take to a catchphrase. Not to mention, it's fed him quite nicely, thank you, over the years.

I look at his face, at the disappointment and condescension there, and realize what a farce it all is. You treat them like princes but the first time you actually need them to put out…they might as well be in insurance.

Faced with this ingratitude, something inside me just gives up.

"Okay," I tell him. "I surrender."

"What?"

"I'll confess, right now. It's the jet ramps, isn't it?"

He looks confused.

"We have this client, a dictator...you know the old joke about, you're not really a country unless you have your own stamps, your own airline and your own beer? Well, he's got commemorative stamps, a brewery, a Mercedes stretch limo and a portrait of himself as Julius Caesar. But he gets embarrassed when his guests have to descend a staircase off the plane.

"There's a staircase on Air Force One' I tell him and he says, 'They could have a ramp if they wanted one.' So when Kumbatta collapsed, we flew a cargo plane in and liberated a couple of jetramps. The guy was so happy, he painted two Cessna's and proclaimed them the national airline. I don't think we *hurt* anybody."

Beltoise settles into the nearest chair, not saying a word.

"That's not it?"

Silence.

"Okay, Napoleon's penis—that was a good deed, I swear."

"*Excusez moi?*"

"It's your Minister of Defence's fault! Not the present Minister, the old one. He had this...thing about Napoleon's penis, that it should be back in France where it belongs."

"It is in France! Napoleon's body is at Les Invalides!"

"The body, sure, but his penis was removed during the autopsy and it's floated around ever since from collector to collector. It's now owned by a urologist, naturally, in Philadelphia."

"Don't be funny."

"It's true. The BBC measured it a few years ago and found it a bit small. Naturally, that outraged the Minister, who insisted the English don't know how to measure. The urologist's price was just *outrageous* so we found a…more generously-sized one around the same age, for a price the Minister could afford. It made him *happy*."

"You found him another penis?"

"Another *old* penis! You think that was easy? How many three-hundred-year-old penises you think are floating around?"

Beltoise stares at me with—I can't tell if it's respect or concern. The odd thing is, to me, this is actually beginning to feel pretty *righteous*. Confession really *is* good for the soul. "Okay, not the answer. Give me a chance. The eighteen identical one-of-a-kind Moroccan emeralds—"

"No."

"The Van Gogh with the wrong ear missing?"

Beltoise rolls his eyes. "We've never met," he warns, "except for a few state dinners with hundreds of other people I've never met either—but my advice is, you find a quick way out of France now. And don't bother replacing your phone—they'll find you as soon as you do. You understand?"

This is terrifying—Beltoise is a glorified flatfoot with a fancy office. I'm *begging* to be arrested and he's not biting. It's *unnatural.*

"Throw me a bone here," I say. "I don't understand what's happened."

He grimaces. "You know damn well it's the bomb."

"The *BOMB?*"

Of course, I know all about the bomb. I'd arrived back in Paris the day before, just in time for the funerals. Twelve dead, 37 injured, a miracle it wasn't more. A mountain of flowers in plastic sleeves heaped on the rubble, candles arrayed like soldiers in front of the dress shop left somehow intact on the corner.

And a march from the *Place De la Republique* to the *Place de la Nacion*, thousands, orderly and dogged, middle-class families and university students, *Le President* and his rivals, butchers, bakers, artists and computer technicians shuffling through neighborhood streets between broad public squares, solemn and chattering, sombre but fashionable—Paris, formal but somehow intimate. Great buildings and beautiful women dressed in black. Paris is a grand dame, maybe a bit past her prime, but she still knows how to put on a funeral.

'It's an escalation,' they say, the voices that multiply in crowds. Just a few years ago, 'they' were content to shoot up a restaurant or concert hall. Now, somehow, they bring in a bomb the size of a safe to bring down half a block of five-story apartment buildings.

The size of the explosion makes people nervous. Nobody builds a bomb that size to bring down the Rue Breguet. We all sense a grander plan that went awry and the fact that no one claimed responsibility only seems to heighten the tension. You don't even have the consolation of knowing who to be afraid of.

Beltoise, however, has made up his mind.

"It's your shipping certificate!" he yells, no longer caring who hears. "Your company's letterhead! Your *signature* on the bloody thing! You think I will cover for *that*, you're insane!"

I stand frozen for an endless moment, until words I never thought I'd hear myself say come tumbling out of my mouth.

"I didn't do *that*! I'm *innocent*!"

And then, I run.

RUNNING

-You ran?

It's an expression. I know better than to run. I walk at my usual quick pace but not fast enough to attract attention. Okay?

I lose myself in the tangle of back streets, staying off the boulevards, sticking to shorter blocks and parks where I can change direction at will. I stop short in front of angled store windows several times, switch direction several more, take a cab for a short distance and then another to double-back on myself. I'm overdoing it, in truth—if GIGN were really on my tail, they'd just throw on the sirens and take me. Once I'm sure I'm not being followed, I find a thrift shop that's just closing in a church, buy a pair of slacks and a short dark hoodie and wear them out of the store.

-This is tradecraft. Where did you acquire your technique?

Like you don't know. I had a very brief career in—what do you tell strangers at parties? About what you do for a living?

-I don't speak of such things.

We used to call it 'compliance.' I was recruited out of college. They trained me to take in a room or a street, to be invisible when that was useful. Trust no one, calculate the odds, tote up the angles and assume everyone follows their own self-interest.

But they couldn't teach me to be shrewd. I got myself involved in an 'extracurricular' scheme supporting freedom fighters—that is, it became extracurricular once it led to screaming headlines. Next thing I know, I'm getting chewed out in front of a Congressional committee for the exact same things they'd urged us to do in private.

We were thrown out like Big Mac wrappers, three fall guys, small potatoes. A generous severance package—under the table, of course—just go quietly into the night, thank you.

That training comes back to me, now that I'm on the run. Focus! *The bomb! What have I got to do with the fucking bomb?*

I need real information. Somewhere in our files, says Beltoise, is a shipping certificate for a bomb with my signature on it. I can't go home so I almost certainly can't go back to the office. But maybe Harry's apartment is clear.

If this had happened any other time—last week, even!—I could have counted on Harry's counsel, his expertise, his instincts. For fifteen years, he's been there when I needed him.

But that's a huge part of what made this feel like the worst day of my life, even before GIGN's visit. I've no idea if I can count on Harry anymore.

-Explain this please. Who is this Harry and why can't you count on him?

Harry is the majordomo, the ringmaster of our circus, the senior partner in Sandler & Son, affectionately known to staff and select members of the governing elite as Swindler & Son. Everything that isn't about Sara in this story is about Harry.

-And Harry's got problems?

Oh hell no, Harry's got no problems. Harry *is* the problem. Everybody *loves* Harry, *that's* the problem.

And why shouldn't they? Harry makes life a party, a twenty-four-hour Remy Martin and shellfish from the little inlet over *there* and put away your business cards, this isn't some vulgar networking grind, we're here to have *fun*! Remember fun? Harry does.

If you liked the Remy, you must try this cognac—it's Venetian, Dante mentioned it (disparagingly, but he mentioned it) in the *Divine Comedy* and let me introduce you to the Ambassador's wife, she has all the good gossip about the orgies at that other embassy—maybe it was the Czechs but we're not saying. Meanwhile, other groups are discussing 70's film and sex robots and if there's anything else you want to know, the person to speak to is over *there*. The band plays good acoustic jazz, the

Argentine tango couple are giving lessons one-on-one on the terrace and the star of the national football club is kicking balls around with enchanted kids and dazzled grownups on the south lawn.

In Paris, of course. That's our home base. It's one of God's jokes—Harry hated the French so, once we'd been thrown out of every other country in Europe, the only place left to go was Paris. Which, of course, he now loves because how can you not love Paris? It's *Paris*, for God's sake.

And the French love Harry. Big gnarly elegant gay Englishman, what's not to love? He ignores their culture, conducts himself like tenth-generation nobility fallen to trade or maybe a good Savile Row tailor, speaks only enough French to be fed and catered to but laughs and charms so naturally, they can't help themselves. Seduction is the French national pastime; they recognize a Master at work.

I was in Mumbai two years ago, picking up a load of Indian cotton. There was a rash of suicides among cotton farmers in Vidarbha and I was able to pick up several farms' entire crop just by paying off the bank loans. I told myself it was a good deed and a good deal. So I'm in the hotel bar at the end of the day chatting up some girl when a man behind me says, "Oh, you work with Harry Sandler? I was in a steeplechase syndicate with him in Ireland once. Took me for £65,000 quid. Most wonderful time I ever had." He bought us both a drink.

Everybody loves Harry; that's what nearly killed us all. As I watched the Iranian commandos lining up on the deck of the ship three hours ago, in their black stocking caps and their Kalashnikovs aimed at our temples, all I could think was, *Everybody loves Harry.*

Fucking goddamn Harry.

Author Biography

Ted Krever watched the Beatles on Ed Sullivan, went to Woodstock (the good one), and graduated Sarah Lawrence College with a useless degree in creative writing.

He spent several decades creating programs for ABC News, CBS, CNN, A&E, Court TV, MTV News, Discovery People and CBS/48 Hours, and as VP/Production of a short-lived dotcom.

He has driven a 16-wheeler across the Rockies, shot overnight news in NY City, managed a revival-house movie theater and married twice, in a triumph of optimism.

He was once accused of attempting to blow up Ethel Kennedy with a Super-8 projector.

Read more at www.tedkrever.com

www.ingramcontent.com/pod-product-compliance
Lightning Source LLC
Chambersburg PA
CBHW020329130626
46549CB00003B/1081